'8 Down' from Saharanpur

By the same author

Earth to Centauri series:
Book 1 The First Journey
Book 2 Alien Hunt
Book 3 Black Hole: Oblivion
Book 4 Civil War (Releasing in 2021)

Short story collections:
Deceptions of Tomorrow: Robots, Black Holes & Time Travel

धरती से सितारों तक:
भाग 1   प्रॉक्सिमा का रहस्य
भाग 2   एलियन हंट
भाग 3   ब्लैक होल विध्वंस
भाग 4   गृह युद्ध
'8 डाउन' सहारनपुर पैसेंजर: उपहास, रहस्य, रोमाँच और दहशत से भरी लघु कहानियाँ

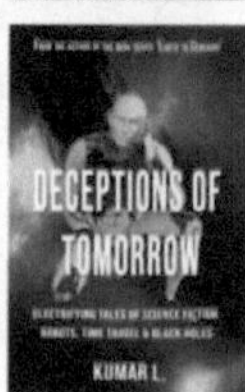

'8 DOWN' FROM SAHARANPUR

&

OTHER STORIES

By

Saurabh (Kumar L.)

WWW.REDKNIGHTBOOKS.COM

Cover design by Aditi Shah (aditicshah01@gmail.com)

ABOUT THE AUTHOR

Whether you want to discuss faster-than-light travel, time travel, black holes or just the latest mobile phone, Kumar is your person.

He is a tech and social media enthusiast. He enjoys travelling and is fluent in several languages. A mechanical engineer who loves pulling apart gadgets and exploring their innards, he writes science fiction stories and tries to bring future technology alive in his books.

The First Journey is the first book of the Earth to Centauri series. It is easy to read and understand and is suitable for all age groups. The First Journey and Alien Hunt, the second book in the series, are both based on themes of adventure, thrill and drama, with a positive outlook at what the future may hold for humanity. Black Hole: Oblivion is the third book in the series with the latest adventure of Captain Anara and her crew.

His books have also been translated and published in Hindi.

You can reach him on
Twitter @Captain_Anara,
Instagram @KumarLAuthor,
www.facebook.com/kumarlauthor

Visit his website www.kumarlauthor.com to learn more.

INSIDE

AN EYE FOR AN EYE

The white cab glided to a stop at the foyer of the hospital. The intense glare of the summer sun cut off abruptly in the shade of the wide porch. But the cacophony of the bustle on the main street reached out to her ears as Aditi opened the door of the taxi and stepped out. Brushing away some dust from her lime green salwar suit, she took a minute to compose herself as the cab drove off. This was the moment. It had taken her over a year, but her plan would culminate today. Her stomach continued to ache - was this due to anxiety, thrill or something else? She didn't really care. Not today.

As she approached the automatic doors welcomed her, and the refreshing blast of cold air sharpened her senses. Ignoring the security guard and the reception desk, she walked across to the elevator bank. She knew her way around well. It was visiting time, so she did not anticipate any problems reaching the room.

The elevator doors opened slowly on the fifth floor, and she turned right without hesitation. Room

506, the sign proclaimed by the side of the door and Aditi slowly pushed it open and looked inside the darkened room. The only light was the soft green glow of the monitors, beeping at regular intervals. The ventilator swooshed softly with every cycle, and the room clearly indicated that death would not be long in coming. She saw her lying supine on the bed.

She stepped inside, carefully closing the door behind her, walked softly up to the bed and perched herself on the right edge, facing the worn visage. As she smoothed her dress, she was rehearsing her speech in her mind. Time was short.

Aditi reached out and grasped the withered right hand lying on the bed, giving it a slight squeeze. It felt cold and clammy, almost repulsive, but she held on. She couldn't allow her distaste to interfere with her purpose.

There was a slight flutter, and her stepmom's frail fingers closed over hers. She opened her eyes, and Aditi could see they were dulled with heavy medication, but the torment of pain was clearly discernible. She tightened her grip and leaned closer so her stepmom would not miss her words.

"Maya!" she called her softly. There was no response.

"Maya!" She raised her voice, while anxiously glancing at the door. Any interruption now would wipe out a year of her carefully prepared plans. Maya turned her head this time and looked directly at her. A grimace of pain crossed Maya's face. There was not much time or life left in her. Aditi would have to work fast.

"Maya, I'm here now, and I have something to tell you," she said and was happy to receive the tiniest nod. She could hear me! Good!

"The time has come to tell you everything, and then you will understand. Whatever I have done is because I loved Dad more than anything else in this world."

"It all started, two years ago with your phone call. Do you remember that call, Maya? I was in Chicago, working for Apex, starting my third year away from home. You sounded hysterical, barely able to articulate anything. I had a feeling then that it was all a show put on for my benefit, but I couldn't be sure. In between the sobs, I was barely able to coax out from you that there had been a terrible accident with Dad. He had drowned while on a fishing trip. I can still feel the numbness as I tried to make sense of the news as my world came crashing down around me."

Aditi's voice almost broke at this point. Hot tears started welling up in her eyes, threatening to break through her carefully controlled facade. She somehow composed herself and continued.

"I barely remember what happened next. The trip back home, seeing Dad for the last time in the coffin, the funeral and the meetings with the police and the rest of the family. Nobody believed this was anything, but an unfortunate accident and it was not until much later that I could connect the dots - Dad did not fish, and he had always been scared of the water - you and I knew this. On top of this, your phoney devastated widow act made me question - what was he doing on a boat that day so far from home, that too all alone?”

Aditi shook her head, recalling the unpleasant memory of that day. “I wish I could have prevented this from happening. I wish I could have saved him. Right now, all I can do is to tell you how he was murdered. Yes, murdered, Maya! He was murdered, and you did it!” Aditi’s chest heaved with emotion as she spoke, the earlier pain replaced by burning anger. “But first let me tell you how it was done and how I worked it all out.”

She squeezed Maya’s hand once more to check she was still awake and lucid and settled herself down a little more on the bed.

“Do you recall the police telling us that they were sure Dad was alone in the boat, and there were enough witnesses who swore that no one else had accompanied him to the village? His cell phone had been damaged in the water, but they'd checked his call records, and except for one call to you that morning, there were no calls or messages to suggest anything out of the ordinary. The police were convinced this was an accident and they closed the case."

"But the niggling doubt in my mind refused to go away, Maya. There was more than what was meeting the eye. I needed more information. So, I went around and spoke to all his friends and colleagues. Unfortunately, they had nothing more to offer. There were some whispers of course, about trouble between the two of you. Whispers, nothing else. Each was shocked by the death but could share no reason to doubt the official version. They'd anyway already moved on with their mundane lives. But how could I live knowing there was more to the death?"

"Desperate for any leads, I decided to dig into his social media accounts. I knew he was somewhat active. I knew the usernames but not the passwords, but I did have a trump card - the SIM from his phone. I put that in my phone and asked for password reset using text codes. I got into all his accounts, and I found a few which seemed really private. And there I discovered this woman he had been talking to. They seemed pretty close, but I had never pictured Dad as a Casanova and that too at his age? The fish smelled fishier so to speak. Especially since her last message was just a day previous to his death and it read - You will go tomorrow but know this, you must come to me, I cannot live without you and death will bring us closer."

Aditi stopped again as the nagging pain in her

stomach returned for a while, then she put it aside.

"I checked out her profile, but there was very little to be gained. I did manage to find that she lived somewhere nearby so on impulse I dropped her a message from dad's account. Of course, there was no reply. But I made it my mission to track her. It took a few days, but you know everything is linked on the 'net. Imagine my surprise when I found the real person was you! You had been talking to him through a fake account, Maya!" Aditi said through gritted teeth, "And it was you who brought him to his death! I know why you killed him too - for his insurance money and you did it oh so cleverly that no one ever suspected a thing. After all, so many people die of drowning. It was just another accident statistic."

"Of course, I could go to the police again, but I did not. No, I decided to take revenge on my own. You had to pay for your sins, and I marked you to die a painful death!"

Aditi was feeling quite calm by this time having got a big load off her chest. But Maya had to know the whole story of how she was paying for her deeds.

"I decided that you had to die a painful death. Simply stabbing you would not be enough though god knows there was enough opportunity for that. You know something funny, Maya?" Aditi continued, "Mercury is one of the strongest poisons known to man, and yet it's available in every medical shop in

India, and best of all you don't even need a prescription! Yes, Maya, it's there in that pretty little thing we keep in our house - the thermometer! I bought dozens of them from shops all across the city, and no one suspected a thing! But I could not just feed it to you. No! That doesn't work. You see it needs to be inhaled to be really effective - the vapours are actually much more deadly!"

"So, I moved out to a hotel, ostensibly to grieve alone, but in reality, I could not bear to live with you in that house. I'd already quit my job so I could devote everything to my master plan. You had to pay for what you'd done!" She stopped to catch her breath, the pain in her stomach seemed to be growing but no matter. This would all be over soon and then she would see a doctor.

"Every few days I'd come and meet you and bring across a bottle of the mercury. I would carefully coat it on hot surfaces in the house - the stove, the back of the microwave, the water heater, even the iron. It took time, it took me many visits and many weeks to ensure you inhaled enough of the poison and I smiled gleefully when you fell sick for the first time. I felt like a master villain!" A small giggle escaped her as Aditi remembered her evil enterprise.

"I kept a watch as your hair started to fall out and you started vomiting blood all the time. I pretended to feed you while I watched you lose weight faster than a starving dog. And I smiled inwardly when the doctors couldn't figure out what was wrong with you. I rubbed my hands in glee; people do that you know when you were finally admitted to the ICU. And today Maya, when you are on your deathbed, I can finally rest knowing I have avenged my father's death!"

Reaching out Aditi slowly stroked the few remaining wisps of hair on Maya's head and whispered, "Goodbye Maya and may you rot in hell!"

Aditi looked down at her for a few seconds ensuring she was still awake and had heard the whole story. It was over. Justice had been delivered.

She got up from the bed strangely empty of feelings and turned away. She never wanted to see Maya's face again. She was a witch, and she had murdered a person. She deserved to die! The more painful the death, the better.

Aditi's eyes widened as Maya gripped her hand back and refused to let go. She turned back slowly expecting this to be her stepmom's last act on Earth but was horrified to see her smile! Maya pulled urgently at her hand, beckoning her closer and something made Aditi go back and sit down again.

Maya managed to pull off her oxygen mask with some difficulty and her voice, when she spoke, was barely a whisper. Aditi leaned in practically next to her lips to hear what she had to say. Of course, nothing Maya said now would make a difference but maybe, just maybe, she deserved this last act of benevolence. "Aditi..." she whispered, the effort resulting in a gasp of pain, but she seemed to gather her strength and continued to speak.

"Yes, I played with your father. I had to ensure he went ahead with the plan and did not chicken out. Yes, I wanted the money. I had given too much in keeping his home and family. But you see I did not kill him." Aditi listened to her mesmerised at this new revelation. "It was your father who killed himself. All for the love of a woman he'd never even met. He was so much in love – the poor fool! I needed to deal him a double blow. There would be no love for him in the afterlife, and I would have his money." Maya's voice grew hoarse, and she struggled to speak. "He wanted me to leave the money to you once he had gone to make up for all the time, he could not support you. But what about me? Men are so foolish. So easy to manipulate. Your father, Aditi, was an idiot."

If the woman on the bed were not already in her last stages, Aditi would have happily squeezed the scrawny neck at that moment. Maya's words no longer mattered. Her father had been a noble person.

For the last time, Maya squeezed Aditi's hand. "My only mistake was in underestimating you but," Maya smiled lopsidedly, evil dripping from her mouth," I do hope you took precautions while spreading the poison. Mercury, after all, is dangerous to everyone," she whispered, and Aditi would swear Maya cackled as she closed her eyes for the last time.

Aditi's face showed her bewilderment as she continued to look down at her stepmother's lifeless face. Then her stomach gave a violent lurch, and Aditi collapsed on the floor, retching blood. Damn that woman, was her last thought, as she lost consciousness, the sound of Maya's cackle still playing in her mind.

BREAD, EGGS & 'MY PLAN'

It was a dark and stormy night. No. That's not how I want to start. I'm just getting ahead of myself. Let's see, it was a Monday morning, and even though the sky was overcast with drizzle, I felt glorious. We'd just closed the deal on the new house on Saturday, making the down payment, now we needed to pay the balance in '240 easy instalments'. Twenty years of servitude was more like it, but still, it felt good. We'd arrived in life. There was order, and I had a plan. Nothing could stop me. I felt great! Being alive was good!

So, on this Monday morning thinking good thoughts, I waved goodbye to The Wife who reminded me to be back early and bring bread and eggs. 'Bread & eggs', really? I was a Senior Manager in one of the largest firms in the City. Which senior manager goes to the market to buy bread and eggs? The elevator was open as I reached it and I realised that this was not necessarily a good thing. The

Liftman sat there with a smirk on his face and gave me a mocking look, apparently having heard the exchange about the 'bread and eggs'. I ignored his proffered greetings and got in, fuming inside.

The lift doors closed behind me as I exited it on the ground floor and made my way to the car, just avoiding the red Mercedes as it pulled out of the space next to mine. Inside was The Banker - sitting pretty with his Gucci sunglasses and Tumi bag in the rear seat, being driven around by a uniformed chauffeur. He waved at me languidly, and I returned it half-heartedly, looking at my Ray-Bans and last year Samsonite as I opened the door of my Honda and dumped my bag inside, somehow folding myself in at the same time. With a clashing of gears and excessive pressing of the accelerator, I exited the gate and immediate ground to a stop in the bumper to bumper traffic. I imagined The Banker stretching back in luxury, reading his morning paper and cursed. Knowing there was no way the traffic was going to cooperate with me this morning, I switched on Nusrat Khan on the player and took a deep breath, settling down for the hours' worth of drive to work.

As I placed myself down on the uncomfortable chair in the office, I thought it might be worth making some changes to my room. It was too cut and dry, a desk, a couple of chairs, a whiteboard. As a senior manager (part of my plan) in the company, I could and should requisition more. Yes, this had to enter into my plan. Along with the upgrade of the house my office would get an upgrade too.

My musings were interrupted by the ringing of the phone. It was The Boss asking me to come over. Now. I quickly checked my emails - no, there was no looming crisis indicated there. What did he want so early in the morning? I had not even been able to get my customary morning cup of tea - hot, sweet and strong. Without that, I would at best be half-functional but guess that would have to wait for now.

I knocked on his door and let myself in. The Boss was alone, and it was bad news. The company headquarters had decided to restructure. I had to find twenty people in my team to be let go by the end of the week. And me? It seemed the company would take calls on senior personnel once the rest was over. Dirty scheming b…. I thought. Get the dirty work done and then get rid of the evidence as well. I just nodded curtly and went out; there was nothing more to be said.

Back to my room and sitting again on the desk. What was the time… just 10 o'clock? The day was shot already. There was a knock at the door, and I looked up. It's Senior Manager 2, in sales. Good looking, reasonably smart. What's up with her? She looks like she's been crying. Yeah, okay she's one of the first to be fired today. We have not been close, but there is some camaraderie. In between sobs, she tells me how she never expected such a thing to happen, and what would she do now. Her husband had been thinking of quitting his job and joining her and now this. I patted her shoulder, gave her some advice, telling her to get her resume polished and send me a copy too. I'll see what I can do. But I think I need to get my resume updated too. When was the last time I'd done that? Just what I needed now. I thought of calling home but pulled my hand away from the phone. No need worrying The Wife for now. So, I now had a new plan - rebuild my resume, start looking for another job.

As I sat there pondering, I glanced across the hall. The Finance Guy was sitting calmly in his room. He did not have my problems, or maybe he's just better at coping. Never seen him flustered or worried. Damn bean counters were heartless anyway. In another day, he'll be off on his Europe tour, sitting in business class, sipping his wine and churning out more reports on how firing more people would make the company more profitable. Who was he to care about the rest of us plebs? And The Finance Guy - he surely would not be buying bread and eggs before heading home. Lucky ba…!

The phone rang again. It was The Manager. The latest shipment was going to be delayed. He needed my help. I agreed to find some time to come over that afternoon. Great! A hundred-kilometre drive was all that I needed today. Why can't these guys manage the plant on their own? I gave up trying to get anything done in office that day and asked for a copy of the organisation chart from HR. It was made available immediately. They were obviously prepared. They must've known about the restructuring beforehand - The HR is evil - I think sarcastically. It feels good to blame someone - The economy, the Prime Minister, HR, Corporate - I went through the whole list as I made a quick trip to the bathroom. Feeling much better having drained myself physically and mentally, I grabbed a cup of tea and made my way back to my car.

As I rolled out the gate, I decided this was the perfect time for sad songs of Jagjit. As the sadness of the first song filled the car, I started feeling low again. I switched it off, better to concentrate on driving. The road was relatively clear now, all minions were in their office, hard at work for The Global Corporate Slave Drivers. Then another thought sobered me up - once my list of twenty was drawn up, I'd be one of the slave drivers too! What the hell? How can one person be in two places at the same time? Heisenberg uncertainty principle floated into my find - we can determine the position or the speed of an electron but not both. Now, why did I think of this now? Must be my engineering background.

A couple of hours later, I pulled into the parking lot of the plant. The Guard at the gate saluted and scrambled to open the gate. I waved back distractedly. Standing around and opening doors, no skills needed except to look a little bit intimidating and sometimes not even that was required. Lucky bas.…

The Manager was unapologetic. For him, all his problems were the result of corporate policies and the gremlins sitting at HQ. I pictured kicking him on his sorry backside and smiled. Maybe I would include him in 'The List'. That would be good payback. At least this hiring mistake I could fix now. The best part was I could take his job if I were laid off. After all, 20 years working in the field had prepared me for something. I cheered up a bit, and for the moment I tried to concentrate on offering some advice and trying to find a solution to the problem at hand. It took all afternoon to work that out, just giving me enough time to grab a bite to eat and looking forward to starting for home. Why did she ask me to come early every day? And what's with the bread and eggs?

It was quite late by the time I started back. No bread and eggs yet. I'll get them closer to home, or maybe I could forget the whole thing! A whole minute passed by while I smiled inwardly at the evil thought before I sobered up. It was not worth a screaming match. I'll get the bread and eggs today.

So now, it was a dark and stormy night. It had

started raining cats and dogs, and visibility was down to a few meters. I switched on my hazard lights and followed the winding road right behind a mini-truck. I looked in the rear-view mirror to find a line behind me. The minions were going home now! Suddenly, there is a crack of lightning right in front! A tree falls on the mini-truck in front, crushing the cabin, just as I remembered - today is Karvachauth. That's why The Wife wanted me home early! Well there would be no moon tonight, and I still did not understand where the bread and eggs fitted in, but right at that moment, I slammed on the brakes.

I thought twice, then opened the door and went out to help. There were others there already. Good to see people helping each other. I went near the cabin. The Driver's leg was trapped - this poor soul was not getting home today in time for Karvachauth - his plan had failed. I tried to help free him. Someone found a crowbar, we combined our strength and pulled him out. He mumbled as he came out - there was a helper with him, but the cabin was empty. Two of us ran to the other side; someone brought a torch. We found another man in the bushes, where he had presumably dragged himself. The two people were put into my car. I volunteered to take them to the hospital. My good deed for the day or maybe even the month.

At last at 10 PM that night, I reached home. As I rang the doorbell, dripping water all over the floor, I remembered - I'd forgotten the bread and eggs. The Wife opened the door - doesn't talk at all. Not a word. This is bad. No this is worse. I tried to explain how I was a superhero that day, saving someone's life. She's not interested. She has remained on a fast since the morning and is this the time that I reach home? I tried telling her about 'The Plan' and the accident. Why should she care? It takes an hour before she consents to break her fast and I can finally go and change. I can feel a cold coming on. I just want to crawl into my bed and die.

Just then my little girl comes over. "Papa," she says pointing to a book, "what does this mean - life as we know it? We can see behind us, but the future is unknown."

As I try and explain the meaning to her, I realise the bitter truth. 'My plan' had failed too. I was never going to be as rich as The Banker or as self-composed as The Finance Guy or even as low in the social pole as the Guard or the Liftman. Life had got in the way. I was going to struggle even to maintain what I had. In one shot The Plan had failed. Just like the lightning which had cleaned out the driver of the truck. Only in my case instead of one moment it had taken one day. I was going to be out of a job very soon. Sighing, I decided to get up and try giving a shot at my resume. Might as well start now. Maybe it is better to go with The Flow rather than with The Plan and see where it takes me.

My phone rang again - only the third time today.

"Hello, sir,' said a professionally sweet voice at the other end, 'I know it's late, but I wonder if this is a good time to talk to you about a Senior Role in the largest firm in the Country? Would you be interested?"

"Darling!" I cried out to my wife, elated, cupping the phone, "I will remember to get the bread and eggs for sure tomorrow."

I had a plan!

SHADOWS AND SILENCE

It was getting very late. Much later than usual. He was getting worried. In the rain-drenched night, all he could see from the balcony was the dark street, a drenched mangy cur and the dark shape of the tree in the yard. Its leaves dripped with water and formed puddles in the ground. There was a sound at the door, and he turned around. It had to be his sister coming back from college - the rain must've delayed her. But why would she knock? She had her own keys.

Then he heard the key turning in the lock and the door was pushed open slowly. Divya entered the room dripping water from the umbrella and shoes on the floor. She looked tired and despondent - another tough day with the students, he guessed. It was always the same story, every single day. His mother would not be far behind he thought and again looked over the balcony, but the road was still deserted. His sister closed the door and went into her room to change, not even looking for him. *That's all right; she will remember me once dinner had been served.*

He wished Divya would find another job. The college was just too far away, and the commute on the local train took its toll. Besides, the pay was abysmal and barely enough for a person to live decently in Mumbai. With his mother's pay as a cleaning woman at the mall, this run-down one room kitchen was all they could afford. His father had died an alcoholic and drained away what little savings his mother had managed to hide away on liquor. Times had always been hard for them, and he could not remember when there had been any laughter in the house.

Divya came back into the kitchen, and he could hear the sound of the latest soap playing on the TV in the next room. That TV was the one luxury they could not do without - a daily escape into the artificial world of the rich and the beautiful. Dinner was always eaten in front of the TV, and then everyone would go off to sleep in the cocoon of their dreams and fears.

Divya's tired features belied her young age. Wisps of dark hair escaped from her tightly tied ponytails. A single red dot on her forehead and a couple of glass bangles on her wrist were all the accessories she ever wore. He remembered when he had brought her the dress many years ago on *Raksha Bandhan*, now so faded that the bright colours had combined into a dull uniform brown. He wished they had some money to buy some new clothes. Three *Diwalis* had gone, and not a single stitch of new garment had entered the house.

The house itself was bleak and damp. A single bulb glowed on one wall trying vainly to keep the darkness at bay. But an overwhelming gloom pervaded the atmosphere and threatened to overcome the feeble attempts of the bulb. The faded white paint peeled in waves off the walls and ceiling, leaving behind a surface as scarred as the skin of a leper. Large patches were visible where the damp had completely worn through. Half-hearted attempts had been made to hide the blemishes with pictures of various deities, such that the whole room looked somewhat like an unfinished temple. A solitary fan, grimy and greasy, rotated slowly, pushing aside the dampness, making a noise which grated the soul. The residents of the house seemed to have given up all efforts beyond makeshift cleaning, letting a home turn into a squalid hovel.

There was another noise at the door revealing a glimpse of broken sandals and then her well-worn saree, one of only three she owned. His mother was home too. Her hair was still in place – well-oiled and tied in a braid. Her stooped shoulders, however, seemed to indicate a burden too heavy to bear and proclaimed her defeat to the world. He was sure the only thing keeping her working was her iron constitution. How long that would hold out could be anyone's guess.

His sister laid down the food while his mother changed. No words were exchanged between them - none were necessary. When life has been throwing misfortunes at you, this is what people end up like - there is no hope and nothing to look forward to. He kept up his watch just to see how long they would take to find him, but they just went about their business. He guessed they thought he was still out – after all he came home much later than this every day; preferring to spend the time with his pals at the street corner.

The TV droned on banally in the background, and the only other sounds were the jarring noise of the fan and the soft clanging as his sister set out the utensils for dinner. There was no table in the house, just a mat which they threw on the floor and sat around, eating. The mat was more to provide a semblance of normalcy than of any practical use. He guessed it did help keep the food slightly away from the cracked floor.

Both of them sat down across from each other, cross-legged on wooden stools. They knew he always liked to sit right in front of the TV and that space was left empty. Divya silently served the dishes of the day - a small cup of *daal*, whatever vegetable available and more importantly affordable and a couple of *chapatis* each, the tastelessness of the food masked by the intense flavour of raw onions and a pinch of salt.

There was a sense of moroseness even in the way the food was listlessly rolled into morsels and pushed to the mouth. How unforgiving could circumstances be when even food turns bitter in the mouth while the stomach desperately craves the sustenance?

'You remember what day it is, Ma?' Divya asked tremulously.

Her mother looked up from her reverie, almost surprised to find someone else in the room with her. The morsel she had been about to put in her mouth remained a few inches from her face. Then a single teardrop formed in her eye and slowly, crossing the deep ridges of her skin, it rolled down her cheek. Even the teardrop seemed almost to give up the effort of crossing the well-worn face, moving with extreme reluctance. Her mother bowed her head and did not answer. But so much meaning was hidden in that single teardrop that a shiver ran down his spine.

His sister stood up and sat down beside her mother. Her own eyes were red and moist. It was only then that he realised, Divya too had been crying in secret, probably the whole day. He almost felt ashamed that he was watching this scene unnoticed, but that was for the best. He did not think they needed to be interrupted by him at that moment.
Divya spread her arm around her mother's shoulder and lowered her head to rest there. The two of them sat there quietly sobbing with pain too deep to

explain. It was almost like someone had burst a boil on your body and was trying to push the pus out and an excruciating pain ran deep inside the body. The pain ran deeper than a few inches, the pain touched the very heart and soul of the person. And still, the pus would never be drained fully. It would keep filling the boil endlessly, raising the ugly head of hurt when least expected.

At that point, for just a fraction of a second, he wanted to reach out and touch his family. He wanted to tell them to be brave and to trust him, and he would make everything alright again. But he held back. An invisible force seemed to hold him, not allowing him to move a muscle. His limbs remained frozen, but his senses were acute - he could hear every teardrop falling from their wet eyes, the slow swaying of the leaves in the rain and the wind and even the shallow rattling breath of the mangy cur on the street. A wave of desperate longing engulfed him and yet he was utterly incapable of making a single movement. Was this the physical effect of his guilt or was it something more profound which he could not comprehend?

He continued to watch the scene playing out in front of him. The two forlorn figures in front of him sat side by side, drawing strength from the other even though there was none to give. He felt a small stab of grief welling up in his own heart, was it because he felt their pain or because in all this time they had not even thought of looking for him? Was he not part of this family too?

After what seemed like infinity, his mother raised her head and wiped her eyes on the edge of her *pallu*. Instead of cleaning up her face it left a dark smear of her *kajal* on her face giving her a sort of macabre look in the dim light. His sister got up too and lovingly wiped the smudge from her mother face. The shared pain seemed to have finally given them some solace if not comfort. Something seemed to beckon him, asking him to go inside and spread a little more hope but his legs still refused to move. *Why didn't they just come into the balcony and guide me back inside?*

His mother got on her feet and moved to the far wall where two portraits hung festooned with dried flowers with an unlit oil lamp below them. There was a time when his mother would light the lamps every evening, but like many other things, that ritual had also been given up in the face of apathy and hopelessness. She gently touched one of the pictures as if trying to relive the memories from long ago. He could almost feel her warm fingers caressing his face as she did so, and he knew the time had come - she would now come to the balcony with some relief and maybe a smile. But she stood rooted to the spot below the photographs and a sudden chill went through her slender frame. She looked through him and towards the tree across the yard, quickly walked across and with a quick movement closed the tattered bedsheet which served as a curtain. With that one gesture, she cut him off from everything that he held dear.

He too looked at the tree in the yard, and he could still see the rope swinging slowly from the branch on the right. It was the same one he had used to hang himself from, three years ago on this day.

13 - TRAYODASHA

There is a faint line dividing sanity and psychosis and I am standing on that line. I am standing on the precipice where I must choose my path; to the left is justice, to the right - vengeance.

I have just woken up in a darkened room. My head throbs. I gingerly probe a bump on the back of my head and my fingers come away with a few drops of blood. I must have been out for a few hours. Sitting up slowly, I peer into the gloom.

I wait in the darkness gathering my thoughts and my strength, looking back at the last three years of my quest, the three years that I had spent searching for the 'Shadow' in the rural hinterland. It had all started with a bloodied male corpse, dumped by the roadside; its throat cut almost surgically, the blood drained away. The rest of the body had been unsullied and covered in vermillion from head to toe. Then we had found the woman, dead of course, on the other end of town, her throat slit in a similar manner. It was only when we found the sixth body that I had begun to see the pattern. A small book in Sanskrit possibly dropped by the killer had been our first and only clue. *Trayodasha*, thirteen, it said on the tattered cover. It was based on some twisted ancient ritual, thirteen deaths to achieve the ultimate power over one's own death. The scholars refused to translate it-it was evil incarnate, they said. They would have nothing to do with it. Nevertheless, I could not ignore such an important lead. I spent all my free time poring over the book, trying to make sense of its message, and in the process, I was drawn so deep into it that it consumed me.

With every body that we found, my suspicions were strengthened. I tried out my reasoning with my superiors but they laughed at me, calling me crazy - there was no psychotic killer loose in this part of the country. Who listens to a town cop? I persisted and got transferred from village to village. Only one person believed me-Rani, my deputy, now posted as a constable in the police lines. Together we pored over the book. We knew that book was our guide to catch the killers.

She was the one who pointed out the similarity between the drawings in the book and the rough vermillion design made on the bodies we had found. A rough *chakra* with a centre point and twelve spokes. We mapped the locations of the bodies and they matched the drawings. Eleven points were full; eleven people were dead before I made the connection. I located the centre, the focal point. The killer had to be there.

I had been waiting at the centre point, outside a rough house made of metal sheets with two possibly three rooms. I thought we would stop them, but they had been smarter. The last thing I remember before I passed out was a sharp blow to my head.

I curse my stupidity in coming here alone. I hope Rani follows my instructions and comes searching for me. I hope she comes in time. The rain falls in waves. I hear it loud and clear, as it falls on the metal roof and runs down into the ground. I am thirsty and hungry. I moisten my cracked lips with my tongue. I wonder if I can lick a few drops of water off the floor. I wonder...

A crack of yellow appears around the edges of what I assume must be the door to my room. Someone had turned on the lights in the next room. Over the noise of the rain, I could just about make out two voices-that gorilla of a man who had attacked me and... a woman. I have finally found her, or, to be more precise, *she* has found *me*. This is not good. I struggle to my feet and with arms outstretched walk around in the darkness until I hit a wall. It seems to be made of metal, but rough and corroded. I find an edge and manage to break off a long, rusted piece. I slip it into my pocket, wiping my hands off on my trousers.

The voices grow silent. I stiffen in anticipation. If

I rush them as soon as the door opens, I might catch them off guard. However, my hopes are dashed when a clear voice rings out through the door, "Step away from the door and don't try anything foolish! Then maybe you'll learn what you have come to find out—the truth. Okay, Mr Kish?" She knows my name! How does she know *my* name? I step away from the door as instructed.

The door opens and I can see her silhouette in the light streaming in from the other room. She pauses at the door, turns around giving instructions to someone I cannot see. "Put the body away with the others. Start the preparations. I will join you." There is a grunt of acknowledgement. A door, presumably the outside door, opens and, for a moment, the sound of the rain streams in. Then, the door shuts with a clang and it is quiet once again. She puts out her hand and flicks a switch, bathing the room with yellow light from a naked bulb hanging from the ceiling. I shield my eyes against the sudden light, and when my vision clears I get my first look at my prison. It can barely be called a room. It must be ten feet by ten at the most. A wooden post in the centre against which I had been lying earlier, a small window, a few empty boxes in the corner and a floor covered with rough cement.

I can see her clearly now. Guessing the age of strange women is not my forte, but I estimate that she cannot be more than thirty years of age. She is dressed in dark slacks and a tee shirt. Several strange bracelets adorn her wrists. Her dark hair is left loose and falls to her shoulders. Her face is expressionless, but her eyes seemed to blaze with some inner rage. It scares me. There is evil emanating from her.

"It must surprise you to see me in the flesh, Kish." Her voice is cold.

I refuse to answer while I walk through the scenarios in my mind. It would have been easy to take her down but for the fact that she holds a gun in her hand. My gun. A .22, but deadly nevertheless in the confined space, and there is no way she will miss me at such a short distance. I pray fervently that Rani has tracked my location and is on her way here.

"Playing the strong, silent cop, are you? Never mind. This will be over soon."

"You won't get away with this," I say. "It is only a matter of time till they find you. You have nowhere to run."

"But you misunderstand me. I never intended to run. My work will be over tonight, right here. You were the last piece. You are thirteen."

"I know all about your book. Nevertheless, your math is off. I'll be number twelve, not thirteen."

Her lips twitch. A cold, soulless smile that does not reach her eyes. "I retrieved my book from your pocket when Aka knocked you out. Moreover, you are wrong. Aka just caught your subordinate hiding in the bushes. She must have followed your cell phone signal or tracking device. A strong young woman. Good thing she was female, you know, she had to be the alternate."

The alternate. Yes, I think. A male, then female, then again a male-the pattern had repeated. Looks like I have finally found the 'Shadow'. The first female serial killer in India.

"Let her go. It is me you want." My voice carries more courage than I feel in my heart.

"A little too late for that, I'm afraid. Like I said, she was alternate. Aka held her down as I cut her throat. She did not even squeal. There is no one coming to help you."

Her words sink in and I scream, a soundless scream. I would have jumped at her, had she not had the gun pointed at me. A dagger appears in her left hand. The blade glints with wickedness as she holds it up by what looks like a heavily ornamented hilt.

"Why? Why would you kill Rani? She wasn't threatening you," I croak. *Not Rani.* My partner and my best friend for the last ten years.

"It was necessary. She was twelve, the penultimate." She holds the gun with one finger and pulls out a small book from the pocket of her slacks. *The* book. "This, Mr Kish, is the supreme weapon. Thirteen sacrifices, male and female, each more powerful than the previous." So, she does not know that I have already read the book threadbare. I know all about her rituals, possibly even more than she does. "The final sacrifice has to be that of my mortal enemy," she continues. "How fortunate that you are here today. But then I have planned this for many years. Once Aka returns after setting her body at the altar, we will put you out of your misery. Sounds good?"

Her matter-of-fact voice is more fearsome than the dagger or the gun in her hands. She is completely unhinged. Nothing can stop her in this dance of death. Except perhaps me. I finger the piece of metal hidden in my pocket, pulling it out yet keeping it out of her sight. I slowly inch forward. This time she does not ask me to stay back. *Why?* I am too lost in my grief to reason it out.

There is a noise behind her. She turns to find Aka standing behind her. "Do you want to finish him off now?"

"No. There is one more thing left to do. Prepare for his sacrifice. Go."

He turns and goes out. As he closes the door, I spring forward, grabbing her by her hair and throwing her off balance. Her gun falls away, yet she does not raise her dagger or make a sound. I turn her over, pinning her to the ground with my body while holding the jagged piece of metal to her throat.

"How about I cut your throat instead?" I hiss.

"You would have already if you'd wanted to." *Why*

the hell is this woman so calm? What am I missing?

"Yes, Kish. Go on. Do it! I know you want to. Do it now! Damn you!"

I take a deep breath, "No. That'll be too easy on you. You must pay for your crimes. A long stint in prison followed by the hangman's noose is what you deserve." My grip on her hair and the metal at her throat remain strong.

"All right then." She sighs. "Then we will do it the hard way." *What now?* She does not move, just keeps speaking, lying against the ground, buried under my weight. "You realise I will just have to start all over again, and what better place than the prison, eh? All those people, all in easy reach, just waiting for me to take my pick. Guards and prisoners alike. Put me in solitary if you like, but I will find a way to get them." She licks her lips. It is seductive and scary at the same time. There is something seriously wrong in her head. "And who knows, maybe we will meet again to finish what we started. *Trayodasha,* Kish." Her voice grows deeper. "Decide now! Will it be me or twelve others?" She licks her lips again and smiles. She has me trapped.

I am standing on the line dividing sanity and psychosis, torn between justice and vengeance, but mostly my helplessness against this psychopath. Hatred swells up inside me; my head feels ready to explode and darkness grows in front of my eyes. She is the reason for three years of hell. She is the reason Rani is dead. She is the reason twelve other people are dead. Mutilated and left by the roadside.

The piece of metal moves a centimetre, then another, and another until I plunge it deep inside the artery on the side of her neck. Bright red blood seeps out slowly at first, and then as the makeshift knife digs in deeper, the blood flows in torrents, drenching me, and puddling up on the rough floor. Her eyes widen and her lips part. She pulls me closer, her voice a whisper.

"There was one other way for me to become stronger beyond even the *Trayodasha*. If I don't kill my enemy, and he kills me instead, as number thirteen. See you soon, Kish." Her voice gurgles and she falls silent.

***

I sit there with her gun in my hand, waiting for Aka to come back, thumbing aimlessly through her book. She has outsmarted me. I am alive but Rani is dead. If the book is correct, she will come back and there will be no stopping her then. But there is a way. There is a hidden message inside the book. A message even she does not know. While she had been out killing, I had been obsessing over the ancient text, pulling out a spell even more powerful than the

Trayodasha.

I look at her body lying there. I have the power to stop her. I take the book under the bulb and peer at the page closely, trying to make out the words. '*Pratilom prabal,*' they said. Stronger in reverse.

'Stronger in reverse'? Can it really work? Thirteen in reverse? Starting with a male?

I am standing on the line dividing sanity and psychosis.

I shift the gun to my left hand, step carefully around the blood pooling on the floor and pull out the knife from her hand. Maybe this will work. It is not enough that she is dead. Yes, I have the power to prevent her from coming back. Yes, maybe I can have all the power the book promises. Maybe I can bring Rani back too.

I switch off the light, open the door a crack and wait for Aka to come back. My first kill was the 'Shadow', my mortal enemy, the second will be Aka and then I will work onwards from there. Thirteen will take some time but I have nothing else to do.

THE VALLEY OF FREEDOM

The air conditioner was on full blast even in the biting cold of December. She wrapped her shawl closer and adjusted her woollen cap. The train sped through verdant fields of sugarcane, interspersed with villages and towns. She knew the train would not stop till they reached Saharanpur in another couple of hours. *Three hours are all I have till we reach Dun, she thought. Three hours to resolve years of resentment. Why did I leave the resolution so late?*

She stared through the fogged windows, random thoughts running through her mind. The sugarcane reminded her of thirty years ago, when her family travelled second class, wrapped up in thick blankets, desperate to get home and snuggle in the even thicker *rajais*. As a child, she always had mixed feelings while returning from the winter vacations with the excitement of time spent at Benaras tempered with the dread of going back to school and facing her five tormentors.

The train crossed a small stream bereft of water but full of round stones and boulders. *We used to cross a similar one when we went to school on foot,* she remembered. And sometimes, in monsoons it would be overflowing, and you had to hold hands to cross safely, without any adult guidance. It was frightening and yet she trusted her elder brother to keep her safe. Then they sent him off to sainik school and she was left without her protective angel.

A few *gur* making sites passed by, steam rising from the boiling sugar cane syrup in the open vats. *Is it my imagination or can I smell the freshly made molasses?* A man rode by on a bicycle, balancing precariously through the narrow path along the side of the railway lines. She remembered the fairs which used to be held in the Dehra of old, before they banned the animal shows and human circuses. That guy who rode a bicycle nonstop for two days. The celebration of Dussehra on Parade Ground and the wooden swords they always bought. And what about that stream that ran right through town? It had been fun dipping our hands in the water which was always cold. Too bad they had covered it all up now and built a road over it.

Dehradun had been wonderful for me as a place to grow up in, if not for the five. Her face clouded over as she remembered how miserable she had been in school. The five were the spoilt, monied brats at her school. Her father had been transferred to Dun and she had been hesitant in entering the large school after the small KV in far-off Assam. They had made fun of her second-hand clothes, handed down from her elder sister, since her parents could only afford one new set of uniforms every year. The patchwork done so carefully by her mother had a way of coming undone at the wrong moments - during assembly or in the playing field. And the five were always there pointing fingers and ensuring no one missed that embarrassing spectacle.

The images still hurt, even after all these years, causing her heart to ache. The fact was that she had endured the taunts, pranks and torment for six long years, having made no friends. As she dragged herself reluctantly out of bed every morning, she wished she were dead. She wished they were dead. However, that was not to be. All of them were alive and kicking today, well into middle age.

Enough, she remonstrated herself. *I must focus on how I will face my adversaries.* It had taken her these many years to drum up enough courage to finally put the ghosts of her past to rest. *I must remain firm and tell them how they had ruined my childhood. I hope they all received my message and will come to Mussourie, the neutral ground.*

The train gave a long whistle as it entered the outer signal and chugged slowly onto platform 1. She decided on a whim, as she got off the Shatabdi at Dehradun that while in Mussourie, she was not going to bond with Riley. With James maybe but definitely not with Riley. James had been the less mean of the lot. She could find it in her heart to forgive him but not the others.

***

The old taxi crawled through the traffic till they reached Rajpur Road and crossed the swanky new mall which had just come up where there used to be forests a few years back. They took the left fork to Mussourie and passed the deer park before starting the climb up the hill. She pushed back the memories forcefully. *I must focus on what I will say when I meet them and not what has passed. The Dehradun I knew will not come back. That was the price we paid for progress.*

The taxi finally ground to a halt at the foyer of the hotel. She had only booked for one night and her return would be by flight. She would get it over with and return as fast as she could to her own home, husband, child and a fulfilling job leading a successful tech business. *I have done well enough. It will be time to rest once I face them off.*

She looked at her watch as she was checked in. *Just enough time to freshen up.* The clerk at the front desk confirmed that the meeting room was ready and waiting for her, set up exactly as she had specified.

***

The six of them sat round the table while two children ran about making noise. She looked around the faces seated across her. None of them looked particularly intimidating or threatening at that time. She was somewhat surprised that they had agreed to the meeting. *I wonder why?* They had spent the first few minutes catching up on where each one was placed.

She mentally evaluated each of them. Cyril looked morose and tired. The bags under his eyes. Married and divorced, she had gathered, paying off alimony and child support. His cheerful manner as a child had disappeared completely. His hair thinned and grey.

Sylvia, so vivacious at fifteen, still had some of the glow left over. The two children were hers and it must have been weary to manage them when her husband was away working out of Dubai.

Riley had been the cruellest of the lot. The meanness still showed in his face. But his face also revealed his bitterness. He had stood for and lost the local elections twice, squandering away his family money in the quest to be famous and powerful. Instead, he had been relegated as a minor functionary in the local office of a large political party.

Clara looked the youngest and was loaded with diamonds and gold. She had married a local businessman. Sylvia had whispered that her husband was having multiple affairs and bought her the jewellery to keep her quiet.

Finally, there was James, the youngest of them with his twinkling eyes. He had been rude to her but not nasty. He had not married and was a senior partner in a finance firm. Well to do and handsome. He looked the fittest and the most comfortable of the lot.

The years had not been kind to her rivals, she decided. Time was always the enemy and always the healer. *Yes, I had spent six terrible childhood years, but they had shaped me as a woman. They gave me the strength to bear loneliness so I could better appreciate companionship. They showed me unkindness so I could better appreciate friendliness. They showed me how people can be heartless so I could better appreciate love. And in return these people are burdened by their own guilt and meanness. They acted out of fear and insecurities because they could not stand someone being better at them at anything.*

This was life. It had shaped her, and it had shaped them. A river flows and it wears away the toughest of rocks and boulders. The round rocks in the dried-up river. Yes, the river had shaped them! Just like it had shaped them, and it has shaped me. Am I happy? What do they see when they look at me? A happy woman or someone who is as tired as them, trying to keep track of her life? Am I really at peace?

She waved away the few queries on why they had all gathered on that day. They accepted her weak explanation - I just wanted to catch up with old classmates.

I cannot pity them any more than they pitied me way back in school. It is not for me to pass judgement or seek closure. I came to seek answers and well, I'll have to be satisfied with whatever I see in front of me. This will be the only closure I will get.

She took a sip from the wine glass in front of her. She would bond with Riley, she decided and with James and everyone else and maybe she could treat them with some empathy if not provide any solace.

'8 DOWN' FROM SAHARANPUR

To say that Muru's bottom was hurting would be an understatement. It was a mass of welts and bruises from the belting he had received from his father earlier that day. He shifted on the cot to try and find a patch of skin that didn't hurt. Failing miserably at finding any such untainted surface he gave up the fight. His tyrant of a father had done a comprehensive job.

He stood up painfully, cursing his father and his fixation on school marks. But he guessed he could expect nothing less from him. His father's own education may have landed him the coveted position of headmaster of the local secondary school of Kakori, but he wanted much better for his only son. Hmph! In his eyes, his father was a failure. He, on the other hand, was sure of his destiny. He was going to be a train driver with the East India Railway Company. His whole life lay in front of him. *Can you imagine a life running the daily passenger between Delhi and Lucknow? Blowing the whistle and pushing in shovelfuls of coal into the boiler. You didn't need to study for that. All you needed was brawn and muscle.*

But as the pain caused by his bruises reminded him, these thoughts could never be uttered aloud. He hated his father and his lack of ambition.

To top it all, this particular night of August was oppressively hot. It had been threatening to rain for many days, but they were yet to see a single drop. To be sure, there were monsoon clouds in the sky today, and they did have good rains in July. His grandfather had continued to declare confidently that the rains would be back soon and with a vengeance and he trusted his grandfather's wisdom. But so far, he had been proven wrong. The rains were needed for more reasons than to just get rid of heat. They were essential if the farmers were to have a good planting season in the coming winter.

He was up on the open roof of their small house at the edge of the village, ostensibly to study but his thoughts wandered everywhere apart from the books. The words had danced before his eyes as he flicked a towel trying to fan himself and drive away the flies. No sooner he would stop swatting than swarms of the little creatures would settle down on every visible part of his skin. He sighed - this was a battle he wasn't going to win tonight. He wished his wife Kala was there with him. He'd seen her only once since their marriage ten months ago. He spent a few blissful minutes thinking of the little girl who had become his wife only to be reminded that she would not be back from her parents' house until he cleared his matriculation. She'd be almost fifteen by then.

He sighed again and gave up on sociology. What was he trying to do anyway? Studying to become a graduate? That would take years! And what would happen then? To become a civil servant, he would have to go to Lucknow to continue his studies. The dream was too big for a school headmaster's son in Kakori. Anyway, none of this was essential or required to become a train driver.

He stood up, disturbing the gang of flies holding a meeting of the League of Nations on the cot. They buzzed around angrily before settling down again in deep discussions. The way they rubbed their front legs looked almost like they were applauding a speaker at the podium. He'd seen the photos of the League in the newspapers - the same black and white overdressed pompous politicians.

He walked to the parapet and wiped his forehead with the sleeve of his kurta. Life was so difficult for a sixteen-year-old in 1925, and the roof of their tiny house was the only place he could get some peace to study.

He looked down into the courtyard below. Mother was trying to relight the cow dung cakes on the stove, occasionally puffing through a pipe to get them to catch fire. The pipe made a whistling sound when she blew through it. Smoke rose from the stove in spirals mixing with the humidity, and there was the familiar sweet yet not unpleasant smell in the air. It was the smell of every village and town in India. His little sisters, all three of them, helped her out, mixing the dough and carefully cutting it into small pieces for the *chapatis*. We'd be getting the girls' married off soon as well.

The flickering light of the second lamp caught his eye. A shadow moved across it, and he drew back hastily. He quickly went back to his books and started reading again, trying to memorise the paragraphs while his upper body moved back and forth in rhythm to his intonation. But tonight, was just not his night. Thankfully a light wind had picked up, and it came as a big relief. He sucked in the cold air gratefully, feeling somewhat refreshed. Perhaps it would finally rain tonight.

The whistle of a train engine pierced the night. That would be the 8 Down from Saharanpur. Late as usual. The railway track passed a few hundred meters from his house, and I knew it would be carrying the day's collections from every station along its route, all the way to the divisional office in Lucknow.

Thousands of Rupees.

He waited for the clickety-clack of the train as it approached nearer. *But there was only silence. Had it stopped? Why? There were no signals till the station which was still two miles away.* He strained himself and could just make out the faint shouting coming from the west.

The night was suddenly torn apart by a sharp report, and then the screaming began. Terrified, he ran down the steps to his mother's side as she and his sisters cowered near the stove. There was a commotion at the door, and his father came out.

"That was a gunshot. Something is happening. Come inside quickly. Now!" He was shouting, and they ran inside without a second thought. He pushed them inside and asked his sisters and mother to hide under the bed. "Keep an eye on them, Muru. I will be right back." He patted his son's shoulder, turned around and walked out the door. Muru quickly shut it behind him, locking the chain. He ran back to his mother, and she caught him in a hug, shaking with fear.

More shouts and screams echoed through the night as they huddled under the bed. He had never heard a gunshot fired before. He had no idea what was happening. He had put off the lamp, and there was complete darkness in the room. His poor sisters whimpered softly. He tried to keep up a brave face, but his legs were shaking like jelly.

Muru didn't know how long they sat in the darkness, straining to hear what was going on outside. Presently some footsteps were heard approaching. There must have been three or four people, and they heard them climb up the stairs to the roof. One person seemed to break away, and Muru heard a soft knock at the door. "Muru, open the door." It was his father. With a surge of relief, he found the strength to get up and unhook the chain. His father stepped in quickly and closed the door behind him.

"Good thing you put off the lamp. Now listen carefully. Everything is all right. I want all of you to stay here for a little while and I will come and tell you when it is safe to come out. Can you do that?"

Muru nodded vigorously, and his father patted his shoulder and went out as fast as he had come in. They heard him again climbing back up the stairs and then soft voices could be heard discussing something in urgent tones. Someone was explaining something, and it felt like a story. Was it about the train and the shot they had heard? Who were the strangers with his father? Muru strained to catch the words as the wind picked them and spread them around. It was a game of hide and seek.

Finally, unable to bear the suspense any longer, he rose up silently, brushing aside his mother's hand as she tried to pull him back down, and walked to the window. He could hear much better now.

"So now you know, Panditji, what has happened tonight. We have been planning this for the last many months, ever since that meeting in Kanpur when we formed the Hindustan Republican Association. You were there with us that day. It is indeed fortunate that we have found you here. If only Guptaji had not fired the pistol by mistake, we would have carried out the robbery and gotten away easily. We only wanted to rob the cash. It would have been a double blow to the British and a shot in the arm for the revolution. We would have proven that we can strike with impunity! And now? Now it is a case of murder!" His voice was agitated, yet it carried immense strength of character.

This was the man in charge. A forceful personality. Then it dawned on me - these people were revolutionaries, fighting against the British. Fighting for the freedom of India. A thrill ran down Muru's back, and he shivered involuntarily.

"We don't know that, Bismilji. That man may still be alive," a second voice spoke up.

"No one can survive a direct shot to the chest, Khan Sahab. Trust me. He is dead. And now we must get away from here immediately. Panditji, can you do something about the wound on Khan Sahab's hand?"

Muru heard someone come down the steps again And enter the courtyard. It must be his father rummaging around in his mother's paltry kitchen pantry for some turmeric for the wound. His father went up again, and there was silence for some time.

The strong voice spoke up again. He had been called Bismilji. Was it the poet and the revolutionary Bismil in our house? All the students admired him and his poems. We had to read them in secret, but he was a legend.

"Do you have something to help us on our way, Panditji? The train will reach the station soon and you can be sure the station master will be telegraphing the police without delay."

"Of course. Of course. You can take my bicycle and I'll see if there is something in the kitchen for you to eat. Where are you planning to go?"

"Agra," said two of them simultaneously.

"And then to Delhi. We need to lie low for some time." It was the voice of the man they had referred to as Khan Sahab.

They all came down the steps, and after some hurried goodbyes, they were gone. Muru's father came back to the room, and Muru unlocked it again. His father sent his mother and sisters back to work but held Muru back.

"I heard everything. Who were those people, father? Were they from the HRA? Are you a revolutionary too?" The words tumbled out of Muru's mouth before he could stop himself.

His father's eyes flashed, and Muru thought he was done for. But he calmed himself and sat Muru down.

"Whatever happens, Muru, you must forget what transpired tonight. Yes, that was Bismilji. He is one of the greatest freedom fighters that I know personally. He told me the whole story. Ten people including him just robbed the 8 Down. One person was shot by mistake, and now they must run because the British Government will hunt them down. This incident, this conspiracy, is a big blow to the ego of the British if not to their coffers."

"Will they be able to escape, father?"

"I don't know. But I wish to God that they escape to carry out their sacred duty to our motherland." He seemed lost in thought for some time, and Muru looked upon him with admiration. His father was a revolutionary! The pain of the belting was forgotten. It was nothing in front of what these revolutionaries were risking - their freedom and their lives. He had been wrong about him all along. Muru's chest swelled with pride. Train driver be damned, he had to follow in his footsteps. Then his father saw him staring and flew into a rage again.

"Don't you have some studying to do, young man? Remember, if I ever hear you speak of this again, I swear to god, I will skin you alive. Now get out!"

***

The police came for his father a few weeks later. He was marched out in handcuffs as a conspirator, but he held his head high. Muru had tears of pride in his eyes, and he'd never admired his father more. His father was sentenced to a year of rigorous punishment, but the key people were hanged eighteen months later.

However, he was now ready to take their place. Instead of driving trains he has started learning about blowing them up. *Sarfaroshi ki tamanna!*

THE WARRIOR

The moon was out in full force tonight. He could see the white jewel as it seemed to hang motionless in the dark sky, overpowering the feeble light of the stars. The moonlight cast the forest in deep shadows and threw everything in deep relief.

It made the river appear as if it had been moulded from silver. It was still the middle of the summer, and the level of water was low. In another two months, the river would overflow its banks, bringing a fresh lot of soil for the farmers to grow their crops. Not that it mattered to him. Like others of his kind, he preferred the jungle to the plains. The trees were his friends, and the animals, his allies.

The gentle lapping of the flowing water was the only sound to be heard in the otherwise still night. The soft hooting of an owl occasionally broke the silence. There was hardly any breeze, and even the leaves on the trees were silent. It was the perfect night for a hunt. But again, that was not his purpose.

He was the designated guard for the night. The King had received intelligence that strangers had been spotted in the jungle. They might be spying for his brother. The King and his soldiers needed to be prepared.

The night had heightened all his senses as he sat high above the ground, hidden in the shadows of the leaves of the neem tree, slowly swinging his tail. He had never felt as alive as tonight. In hindsight, that should have been one of the first clues. The night was too perfect, too pristine. It was uncanny and as he watched the placid waves of the river, mesmerised by the scene he distinctly heard the sound of approaching footsteps.

He turned his head slowly to follow the source of the sound. He watched as two figures slowly came into view. He could only see bare silhouettes of the two men as they stepped out of the jungle and made their way towards the river. It took a few minutes before he could finally make out more details about them. Both of them seemed to be dressed in simple ascetic clothing, carrying cloth bags in their hands but they seemed too young to be ascetics. Their tall athletic built, their muscular torsos and the shape of the long bows they carried slung casually over their shoulders belied their simple appearance, as also the naked swords hanging at their waist. Their backs were towards him and try as he might he could not see their faces from his perch. He thought of changing his position to get a better view but restrained himself. It would not do to spook the strangers until he could determine their intentions. Why were they here so deep in the forest, far from any village or *ashram*? Were they spies against his King or innocent hunters, just out to track animals?

One of the two walked to the bank of the river. He brought out a wooden jug from his bag and filled it with water. He walked back and offered the jug to his companion with folded hands. The other person gracefully accepted the water and drank his fill, returning the jug back. Observing the deferential attitude of the first man towards the second, he assumed that was the elder or the more senior.

The two of them set about collecting dried wood from the base of the trees and carrying them near the river bank, presumably to build a fire. A sensible precaution. The jungle was full of wild animals and the nights, even in the middle of summer, could be quite cold. Very soon the warm glow of a roaring fire lit up the night and they sat cross-legged next to each other.

Their backs were still to him and it troubled him that he still could not make out their faces. They started speaking in low voices while passing some fruit to each other. At this his stomach seemed to give a grumble, painfully reminding him that he had not eaten anything for the last two hours. Two hours equalled a lifetime for him. After all, he had once almost managed to eat the Sun. He decided his hunger would have to wait. He needed to find out more about these warrior-ascetics. Slowly getting up from the branch, he climbed down the tree, being very careful not to step on any dry twigs or making any other sound. Silently, He crept closer to the edge of the tree line and crouched behind a dune, stopping to listen to them speak.

He could make out a few words from where he was hidden. Their tones were almost lyrical, their conversation like a story. Lost love, missing family and a very long journey. He had to learn more. He needed to take the chance. There was something ethereal about the whole scene. Something seemed to tug at his heart, begging him, pushing him to go closer. It was imperative that he hears the story. It was crucial that he find out more about them. This was the time that he had been waiting for his whole life. His destiny awaited him.

He moved closer, almost slithering on his stomach till he was but a few feet away, silently becoming one with the sand, and hardly daring to breathe. He could hear better now. The younger one was cajoling his companion - they had to move faster if they were to have any chance of success. They needed to prepare for a battle. No. Not a battle, a war. They had to prepare for *the* war. The war to end all wars. They had already spent years in the jungle searching for clues. They needed more allies. They needed an army if they were to defeat the enemies and carry out the rescue. Righteousness was on their side. Truth was on their side. God was on their side.

He was finally close enough to see their faces. His breath caught in his chest and he was transfixed by the radiance on their faces which showed through even through the pain they were obviously feeling. He felt as if he had looked directly into the sun and was going to be blinded with the radiance. But still, he was unable to tear his eyes away. There was no way these two were human. A small sob finally broke through his consciousness, and he returned to reality.

As they continued to reminisce, he could personally feel the pain the elder one was suffering from. His heart went out to the elder man. Tears filled his eyes, and his vision grew bleary. These people were no spies. They were not the enemy. They needed his help. They needed his King who had been wronged too. Together they would be a formidable force. Together they would defeat the evil which had cast a dark shadow on the land. All evil was connected. They needed to defeat one to weaken the other.

The younger one had finally stopped speaking. He reached out and laid a hand on the shoulder of his companion whose chest seemed to be heaving with emotion. What was the bond between these two men? The elder one raised his eyes and smiled back tentatively. His eyes hardened as he seemed to find his resolve and his face transformed. The radiance was back again, and it was stronger than ever.

He forgot everything. He forgot his birth. He forgot his King. He forgot his duty. He forgot the circumstances which had forced him and his brothers to live in the jungles. He was overwhelmed by an indescribable emotion, and his legs were paralysed. Only one thought kept repeating in his mind - He had to meet his saviour. He had to fall at his feet and seek deliverance. Only he could relive this burden which he had been carrying for so many years. He would serve the elder and offer his life in exchange for salvation.

Somehow, he managed to pull himself up on his feet and stagger forward. His hands were folded, his face was awash with tears, and the tail swung slowly behind him. And yet, he managed to smile. The younger person turned around swiftly at the sound of approaching footsteps and drew his sword with a rapidity which was incredible. The terrible blade on the sword glinted wickedly in the moonlight and rage had transformed his face. But he was beyond fear. He had eyes only for his Lord. He stumbled forward and fell on his knees. No words could escape his mouth, and he slowly swayed where he had fallen. It did not matter even if he had died by the sword at that time. He was ready. He was prepared to die at the hands of his Lord.

A pair of hands gently touched his shoulders and pulled him to his feet. He could not raise his eyes to look into that face. He felt weak, lifeless. His limbs hung useless at his side, like those of a rag doll. His Lord had recognised him.

"I am your humble servant my Lord. I have waited for aeons to meet you, and from this day onwards I will only serve you. Your smallest need will be my command, and I will lay down my life before I allow an enemy even to touch your shadow."

The elder brother smiled as he pulled him close and embraced him. His very soul was filled with happiness as the radiance seemed to warm the very core of his body. He had arrived. He was home.

SHAAPIT: THE 'CURSED'

"Settle down, girls," I hollered from the front seat for the umpteenth time. There was a momentary pause in the screaming from the back seat, and my wife grunted in her sleep. I knew the peace would not last, but I needed a few minutes of peace. My nerves were seriously on the edge. The throbbing in my head was getting worse, a combination of lack of sleep and the length of the drive. I massaged my right temple, trying to relieve some of the constriction. It felt a little better.

Outside, the sunshine and the greenery belied the dangerous times. The road was clear as I'd expected but the surface was well worn. No movement of any groups of undead had been reported in our city or our destination. The route had been clear; I'd checked it last night, in the morning today, before getting into the car and every ten minutes since then. Nothing. Small comfort. I still did not understand why this trip was necessary. We'd not set foot outside the city in the last five years. It was just too dangerous. But the grandparents had not seen our elder daughter in the previous five years and they'd never met the younger one at all, so this was a chance we'd decided to take. God knew if there would be another opportunity.

The 'disease' or 'curse' as everyone had taken to call it had risen out of nowhere. Whole cities, towns and villages had been overrun before the army, and the air force had managed to contain the spread by carpet bombing and clearing out entire swathes of land. We now lived in human-made islands only connected by air or through the monthly convoys which moved at high-speed protected by aircraft. Anyway, like citizens of a nation in a state of war, we'd also learnt to live in the face of constant danger.

I stole a glance at my wife in the front seat. She was deeply asleep, her head lolling a little with the motion of the car, dark goggles slightly askew on her face. I envied her ability to sleep in moving vehicles. Me - I had never managed to shut my eyes in peace while encased in any moving object, including and not limited to cars, buses, trains and aeroplanes.

The girls had started bickering again, causing me to emit a long sigh. I did not even bother to scold them again, just turned up the volume on the FM. The speedometer held steady at a hundred. It was a pity the safest airport was so far away from my parent's house. The few cars and trucks we did come across scooted away from us, as if we had a sign painted on our side - 'Danger - *Shaapit* on board'. But you couldn't blame them. They'd learnt to be careful – more often than not the hard way.

The last army barrier was many miles behind us, and we'd cross many more before our journey ended. Another hour or so, I did the calculation quickly in my head. We should be just in time for lunch and plenty of time before it gets dark. Not that reaching early guaranteed safety. I cursed myself silently for not carrying any weapons for the trip, but they still did not allow guns on aircraft, and there had been no time between landing and picking up the rental car to find a gun shop. This was supposed to be a short trip, and there was no need to frighten the girls by loading the car with weapons. The tyre iron in the boot would have to do in a pinch.

We passed a sign warning us about the approaching security barrier. There were plenty of warning signs now. The government was spreading the word freely - the 'cursed' could not read after all. I squinted against the bright sun as this barrier came into view in the distance. There was something different about this one. For one, it was bigger than anything we'd seen earlier. Tanks parked on the side, armoured personnel carriers, machine guns and what looked to me like a hundred soldiers.

"Something's happening," I muttered to myself as

I reduced speed and came to a stop right at the barrier. I ran a wary eye at this overt display of military might, not sure if I should be frightened or relieved. The girls had their faces stuck to the window, goggling at the spectacle outside, their pretty hair all done up in braids and tied up with red and blue ribbons. Lord, I loved them so much, so help me.

I rolled down the window as an officer walked up to the car, looking dead serious in black combat clothes, carrying a rifle slung over his right shoulder.

"Is everything all right, officer? What's the matter" I asked him.

"Routine check, sir." His voice was deep with a hint of southern accent. 'Unni' said his badge. "Are you going far?"

"Just on our way to Tal."

"Uh huh. You're going to stick to the highway, right?"

"All the way, officer. Shortest way, you know. Is something wrong? Haven't seen so many troops in one place today."

"Nothing to worry about, I'm sure. Try going a little faster, will you?"

His voice was calm and measured, but I could see his fingers move nervously over the trigger of his gun. Something was definitely off. 'Don't worry' be damned, I was ready to shit my pants. But before I could probe any further, the barrier opened, and he waved us through.

As the car picked up speed, I heard a sound like a swarm of angry hornets and shortly, a whole bunch of helicopters passed overhead, heading back the way we'd come.

That was all the encouragement I needed to floor the accelerator. The car jumped like a wild horse, and there was an immediate howl of protest from the back seat as the girls presumably fell off the seats.

My wife had woken up, of course, and once she'd raised her sunglasses and determined that there were no broken bones in the rear, she turned her accusing eyes on me.

"What are you trying to do? Slow down, will you."

"No time. Check the radio. We need to know what's happening."

"Did the army man say something?"

"He didn't, but they were all nervous. Did you notice that none of the soldiers was slacking off? They were getting ready for a face off. And those helicopters? It can only mean one thing."

That perked her up. She fiddled with the knobs on the radio to get the news.

A disembodied emotionless voice drifted out. "..there have been confirmed reports of large scale movement of the 'cursed' near Tal valley. Army units have been mobilised to counter the threat. Martial law is now in effect in the entire district. Curfew is in one hour. Full CPP1 is in place. This is not a drill. There have…"

"Damn!" I said before I could help it. CPP1 - Cursed Prevention Protocol 1 was the highest level of emergency. "Anything on the groups?" I asked my wife. I turned slightly and looked at the girls. "Get your seatbelts on." I tried to keep my voice calm, but the command came out almost in a whisper. "It's gonna get bumpy. Do it." Slightly better. They must've sensed that something was not right for they obeyed without question.

They were only five and eight, but everyone knew about the 'curse'. For god's sake, last year it had been included in the primary school curriculum. No one knew how the disease had started just that it spread through biting. The virus thrived in human saliva. Once bitten you got one maybe two hours before you also turned into what had earlier been called 'a zombie'. Of course, this was predicated on the fact that you had not been eaten alive first. It was a horrible death and an even worse way to live. The 'cursed' roamed around aimlessly looking for prey or waiting to get killed by a bullet. In the safe cities, we'd learnt to try and live as normal as possible, pretending there was nothing beyond the burnt-out land waiting to emerge and wipe us out. It was only a matter of time. We would be pieces of rotting flesh very soon. But for now, we lived our mundane lives.

My wife scanned her phone. "Nothing. No warning. No rumours. Nothing." She was frightened too.

I did not answer as I concentrated on keeping the car away from the edges as it careened around the curves. We'd just begun climbing the hill which led into Tal valley. There was an army base there. We'd be safe in Tal. This, I knew, was more to shore up my own courage than any real hope. Everyone - us, the army men, and my parents - we were already dead. There would be no escape.

"The news might not have spread back home. Or.."

"Or?"

"Or everyone back home is already dead." My voice was flat and low. "We need weapons."

She visibly blanched. Not a coward in any sense of the word, she knew very well - armed or not - the four of us would not stand a chance against a horde.

The car raced ahead eating up the road steadily as we all sat in silence with our own thoughts. We crossed the temple at the top of the hill, narrowly missing a mongrel strolling jauntily across the road. It ran away, howling, it's tail between its legs. An odd thought - scientists had determined that animals were not affected by the disease even when bitten. The specifics were still not known, but all scientists worth their name were out on the track. As a result, wild and tame animals were disappearing faster than you could say 'Bob's your uncle' - trapped, tested on, and then killed off. The forests were bare, and we were no closer to finding the antidote or vaccine.

As we crested the hill, the outer village came into view, and though the streets were quite deserted, there were a couple of shops still open. My eyes lit up. With a squeal of tyres, I twisted the wheel and ground to a stop in front of a promising looking hardware store.

"Stay here," I ordered, "and lock the doors. I'll leave the engine running." I jumped out and only partly heard the door lock behind me. I looked back and nodded approvingly. She nodded back hesitatingly. My elder daughter screamed for me, but there was no time.

Long ago we'd discussed our plans if we ever faced such an eventuality. It was to be every person for themselves - one child each was to be managed. Survival would be the key.

The shop was a real stroke of luck. It had everything I would need. Without bothering to greet the owner, I ran straight to the displays randomly picking knives, axes and hammers. No guns of course. That would have been too much to hope for.

The 'whoop whoop' of the siren nearly made me jump out of my skin, and I dropped my armload on the floor with a clatter. We were *really* running out of time. I picked up whatever I could. The shopkeeper had disappeared, and I did not bother with him or with paying for the goods I'd appropriated.

I ran back to the car, jumping clean across the steps at the entrance, wildly gesturing to my wife to unlock the doors. I pulled up the boot and dumped my 'arsenal' on top of the suitcases. Then, almost as an afterthought, I picked up an axe and a knife and shut the boot with a bang, ran to the driver's side. Dumping the axe and knife in my wife's lap, I shifted gears, and we were back on our way. The sirens continued to whoop mournfully around us.

Just a few more minutes and we'd be in the relative safety of a house. But the going was tough, with abandoned cars blocking the road. Bags, shoes, carts, even school bags lay all around. Hardly anyone was to be seen around. Deciding we might make better time using the side roads, I took a hard right and then a left, coming out on open ground. The car bounced on the uneven land and stones and dust flew all around us. I was afraid of getting a flat but again this was not the moment to ponder on what could happen. Just across was the backstreet leading to my parents' house and with another violent twist of the steering, we were on a relatively clear road. The sound of the sirens seemed to fade a bit as we entered the tree-lined street. It was completely deserted. Not a soul in sight though we did spy a couple of white faces peering fearfully behind drawn curtains.

The car juddered to a halt right in front of the black iron gates of my parent's house. We jumped out from either side, and while my wife grabbed the kids, I raced to the boot, grabbed the 'weapons' and followed them inside. My father was waiting for us just inside the gate. He pushed us in and closed the gate behind us. He shuffled up behind, and we fell inside the side door which banged shut behind us. There was a rattling of bolts and chains as my father locked it securely. I did not bother to look up for a few seconds, still trying to catch my breath, until I realised, I'd left the car running. I should probably go back and shut it off. I managed to get up and started for the door.

"Gotta turn the engine off."

"Are you nuts? No one's going out now. Sit down." Two pairs of hands grabbed me. My father could be quite active despite his frail appearance, and my wife had the grip of a woman possessed.

"Ok, ok. You don't have to crush my arms," I said testily, rubbing my left arm and letting go of the door handle. I didn't think it was a good idea to go out again anyway but giving in to them meant avoiding looking like a wimp.

My heart was thumping away at the speed of a locomotive as I looked around the five people in the room. Two kids, two oldies and one scared woman. There was no way we could fight off the mass of bodies assembling somewhere very near. It was hopeless.

The sirens continued to wail outside, but there was another more ominous noise steadily growing louder - as if a river had been let loose from a dam. It must be thousands if not hundreds of thousands of the 'cursed' outside. I dread filled my heart, and my legs threatened to buckle out from under me.

The girls started crying again. Kids have a strange way, you know, of channelling their parent's feelings and I sure was not helping standing there scared shitless. My wife and mother gathered the kids in their arms, and I somehow managed to push them to a corner. They sank down to the floor. My father and I kept standing. There really wasn't much we could do.

"You gonna hold on to all of those? How about sharing a knife with me?"

I handed over a knife to him somewhat sheepishly. "Sure you can use it?"

"Do I have a choice, son?"

At that moment I admired his calmness more than ever before. Isn't strange how you realise the value of a person when the end is finally near?

There was the vicious sound of a rifle shot outside immediately followed by a staccato report of a machine gun. The army had finally engaged the 'cursed'. Something snapped inside me, and I suddenly felt the cold handle of the axe in my hand. Its weight gave me a little bit more of strength and the last moment of clarity.

"We have to secure the house."

"Done that. Everything's locked and bolted."

I nodded. That would buy us some time.

The sirens stopped. So also did the firing which had continued till that time. There was a pause, and the silence seemed deafening until broken again by muffled sobs.

"Are we going to die, Mommy?"

"Hush child. No one's going to die." The desperate look in her eyes said otherwise as my wife buried her face in my daughter's hair, still tied in a ponytail with red ribbons.

Then the banging and breaking and screaming began. What started off as a couple of people screaming in pain rose to a crescendo until it felt as if hundreds of animals were being slaughtered. Not just being cut in pieces but being eviscerated or burnt alive. There was also an odd sound of hundreds of shuffling feet and demonic guttural tones. The bitter nauseating smell of rotting flesh and fresh blood flowed through the gaps between the doors and windows causing me to gag. Have you ever smelled a dead rat or a dog on the road? This was exactly like that except a hundred times worse. You can never forget that. It becomes forever etched in your memory. We were going to die. Horribly. My sweet daughters. My wife. My parents. Me. The old and the young. We were all going to die together.

This realisation gives you an amazing clarity of the mind. They say the mind is sharpest just before death. I suppose you would not understand this till you are at your deathbed.

Something banged against the gate. Then a few more. The rattling grew louder, and we could hear bodies climbing over the gate and falling inside. A mewling sound followed this - like cats or chalk screeching across a blackboard. More noises. Slithering, shuffling. The smell was even more pronounced now. Hundreds of dead and yet undead bodies. I could imagine their features or lack of it – half-eaten or rotting flesh hanging off exposed bleached bones, hollow sockets where the eyes should be, open sores in place of the nose and disgusting liquids dribbling down the mouth and chin. Do you get the picture?

Shadows crossed outside the closed windows. The windows rattled.

We were absolutely quiet inside. Even the girls were silent. I looked over. They'd all fainted. I guess that was as good as anything else. I didn't know how long I would be able to stand it myself. Maybe fainting was God's way of having mercy on us. I'd never felt such an intense wave of fear before. Ever get up in the middle of the night and felt that there was someone else in the room watching over you? Now replace that one shadow with hundreds. It was much worse than that. I realised the real meaning of the phrase 'his blood ran cold'.

It was said that they could smell live humans better than dogs. Nobody knew for sure, but this would be the time we would find out. Anyway, with the room dark and quiet maybe they would not notice us, give up and move on.

That hope died as suddenly as it was born. Something hit the door like a battering ram. I could also hear something climb up the window ledges - probably trying to get to the roof. I screamed then. I screamed louder than I'd ever screamed before. All reason had left me. I don't remember much. My senses seemed to have blacked out.

The door shook again but held. I closed my mouth with an intense effort ashamed of my cowardice. But my body refused to let go of fear. Whatever was outside would show no remorse, no regret. They had no feelings. They had no souls. We could not expect any mercy.

The screaming outside was petering out, but the door kept shaking from the pressure of a hundred bodies. More bodies climbing up.

"Are you sure everything is locked?" I asked my father who was still as a statue. He nodded in answer.

"What about the skylight? How did you secure that?"

He looked back at me with blank eyes. Seemed as if the old man's calmness had finally been shattered.

"Oh God, you forgot about that, didn't you?"

I had to get up there. That was the only weak point right now. I looked back at my wife and daughters, ran a hand over their heads and turned towards the stairs. That was the last time I saw all of them alive.

I reached the top just in time to be plastered by breaking glass as the skylight shattered and bodies fell down twenty feet to the floor below. They just did not stop, and hundreds of them kept entering and falling through, many of them now falling on the landing where I stood. The side door also splintered at the same moment. I'd been wrong about the house being our protection. I'd been wrong about so many things today - my preparedness and my courage were on top of the list. I'd let my family down.

There was no more time for any other thoughts as I raised and brought down my axe at the mass of 'zombies' in front of me. The herd ignored my feeble attempts, and such was the size of the horde that I was simply trampled where I stood. My head hit the floor hard, and I felt my left arm break. Somehow, they all ignored me and ran pell-mell down the stairs. Perhaps the fresh meat below was more attractive. Why was I spared further pain I simply do not know.

I lay there on the landing being crushed under shuffling flailing legs until I could hardly breathe. They moved down in droves and through clouded senses I could hear my family screaming. I could do nothing. Believe me, I tried. I tried, but I was held helpless, pressed against the hard, cold floor, completely unable to move. There is nothing worse than the sound of your children being torn to shreds and their screams of helplessness. I cried in silence as hot tears rolled down my cheeks.

The flow of the 'cursed' ceased. I turned my head and crawled to the edge. All I could see was a mass of bodies and a lot of blood. Fresh blood. Blood running in rivulets across the floor and a glimpse of a pretty head with the hair in a ponytail tied with a red ribbon nearly severed from its body. Then the mass moved together until there was no one and nothing left in the room. They were gone.

I don't remember much about what happened afterwards. I seemed to have crawled out of the house after many hours, dragging myself to the car, relieved that it was running and made my way to the hills.

Day 6

It has been six days since I escaped the massacre. My left arm hangs uselessly by my side, somehow held in place by a few scraps of cloth I'd managed to scavenge. The pain doesn't bother me much anymore, but there is another smell. I think its gangrene. Not that it matters. I'll be dead soon too. That undead smell is everywhere now. I can smell it from miles away carried on the gentle breeze.

I had managed to make two trips into town. Once to get some food and water. Second to reconnoitre. I found a pistol that first time. It was just lying on the street with a full clip of bullets. I tried putting the barrel into my mouth and pulling the trigger. I couldn't do it. I was still a coward that day.

The second time I'd found my family. What was left of them anyway. Cursed. I recognised the red and blue ribbons. They were all in the same group walking around aimlessly, the smell of rotting flesh following them everywhere. They were missing limbs, and their intestines dragged on the ground behind them. Soulless, sightless eyes stared straight ahead, unblinking.

But I am stronger now. I think I have enough courage left to do what is important. Tomorrow I am going into the town again. I'm going to find them, and then I'll put a bullet in their head. After that, I will put the gun into my mouth. I can do it now. I'm sure.

That will be my salvation.

To whoever finds this diary - I am sorry. Pray for my soul, and I hope the 'cursed' do not find you.

THE CON - A BAGFUL OF MONEY

There was a spring in my step as I navigated the Sunday crowds. This would be the grandest job I ever planned and possibly the last one I would need to pull off. If all went well, I would be off the grid in a few hours. There was, of course, the minor complication of my wife, but I had a plan for that. Life's like that. I win, others lose.

I walked past old, squalid buildings in the growing evening gloom, refusing to let the cacophony of horns from the barely moving traffic interrupt my singular focus on the task at hand. Anyone looking my way—and no one was—would see a non-descript middle-aged man in fawn trousers and a dark blue shirt, someone who wouldn't warrant a second glance. My sleeve carefully covered my only indulgence: a gold and silver Rolex, stolen not bought. I yearned for the day I could flaunt it openly. Hopefully, it wasn't far off.

I spotted the cafe a few meters away. I was a few

minutes late for our meeting but that, of course, was just as I had planned it. Let the mark sweat. It would make him easier to deal with.

I climbed the two small steps and pushed the door open. There was a couple sitting in the cafe when I walked in. It was dark inside and I nearly missed the couple sitting in a booth by the side. They turned and I realised one of them was Tar, my wife. It was only thanks to years of practice that not even a hint of surprise showed on my face. That particular skill was fully taxed, though, when I saw who her companion was. Sai! What was Tara doing with the mark?

Without breaking stride, I made my way over to their booth, briefly nodding to Rajan, behind the counter. Our eyes met, and I silently accused him of letting me down. The sheepish look in Rajan's eyes should have been my first clue that this meeting would not go the way I had planned.

"Tara? Fancy meeting you here. I thought you'd be at home." My tone was bland but my eyes blazed. Her time was up. I could no longer allow her to interfere. She would have to go. I turned to the mark. "Good to see you, Sai. Sorry, I kept you waiting." I slipped into the sofa next to Tara. My eyes had already spotted the maroon bag on the floor beside Sai's leg. The prize.

"Absolutely all right, Dev. We've only been here a short time. Your wife has been kind enough to share the details of your proposal with me. She said she came over to keep me company in case you were late."

"Oh, she did, did she?" I glanced at her, but she was pointedly sipping her coffee, refusing to meet my eyes. What was her game? Had she revealed my con to Sai? If so, I had just landed in a whole lot of trouble. I decided to play it by the ear and turned to Sai. "Well, we are short of time and there are many people interested in the proposal, as I had mentioned earlier. Have you decided?"

"Of course. I am ready as soon as you can show me the diamonds."

I studied him carefully as I reached into my pocket, pulled out a small cloth pouch and poured the contents out on the table. The sparkle of the small rocks matched the glitter in Sai's eyes as he reached forward eagerly and picked one up, examining it carefully. The greed in his eyes convinced me—the man knew nothing; he was as gullible as ever. Tara's motive in coming here was not to ruin the con, but to make sure I didn't make off with the cash alone. Damn her! Her presence here would mean a little change in my plans for her, but no matter, I could always deal with her later.

"They are as perfect as you said they would be, Dev. Looks like we have a deal. I have your fifty lakhs right here with me." Sai patted the bag at his feet.

I smiled back at him. Collecting the rocks, including the one in his hand, I put them in the bag, closed and palmed it. I slipped it off the table and, with one swift movement, replaced it with the second one I was carrying in my pocket. I would pawn the originals off the same night.

"Anything else I can get for you?"

I almost started. Damn. I had allowed the waiter to sneak up on me. Rajan stood at Sai's side and looked at us, expectantly.

I was just waving him away when Tara piped up, "The coffee is really good. I'll have another cup, please." I shot her a glare, but she shrugged. "I have to use the restroom anyway. The coffee will come by then." She got up with a flourish, and her hand swept a spoon off the table. I clicked my tongue in irritation. Dumb woman, always blundering abound. What had I ever seen in her!

Rajan bent to retrieve the spoon, as Tara nonchalantly squeezed past me out of the booth, nearly squishing me with her hips in the process. I had to fight down my irritation when I caught the damn mark hiding a smirk. I forced myself to focus. Fifty lakhs. That is all that mattered.

"Don't take long, your coffee will get cold," I called after Tara, sarcastically.

I wanted to get out of here fast, now that the deal was done. But there was no way I was going to leave Tara alone with Sai. She knew too much. She could ruin everything if she thought I'd made away with the money.

"You wouldn't mind telling me how you get such magnificent stones at throwaway prices, would you?" Sai said, intruding into my thoughts.

"Trade secrets, Sai. You don't ask how I get them, and I won't ask what you do with them."

"Of course. Of course." He gave me a toothy grin. "But let me say I am delighted to have made your acquaintance, Dev. Ever since you approached me on FB, I knew we would do profitable business together. So, it looks like it's time to close our deal. Unless, you want to wait for your wife?"

"No, let's proceed. Here you go," I said as I handed over the pouch with the fake diamonds and received the maroon bag in return. Fifty big ones! I hefted the bag feeling its reassuring weight.

The door opened just then, and a couple of cops walked in. They came straight to our table as if they knew precisely who they were looking for.

"Did you inform the police about our deal?" I hissed at Sai.

"It wasn't me, I swear to God!" His voice betrayed his panic.

"Which one of you is Dev?" The first cop asked without preamble. "C'mon. C'mon, we haven't got all day."

"That would be me." I tried to remain impassive. It would be at least five years if they found the stones on me.

"You are under arrest for suspected dealing in stolen diamonds," the cop replied as he ruffled through my pockets and bought out the pouch with the original diamonds.

"Hey, wait a minute!" shouted Sai. "Then what are these?" He brought out his own pouch and emptied it on the table.

"Fakes, I would assume," said the policeman.

"You double-crossing son-of-a—!" Sai's face was red with fury.

"Open the bag," the cop ordered next.

I complied quietly. Diamonds gone, and now the cash. What rotten luck! I wondered who had ratted me out. I pulled out a few wads. They were just scraps of paper. I wanted to laugh out loud. I threw one at Sai. "Here's your cursed money, Sai. Looks like she got us both!" I rummaged around inside the bag and found a note. "May I?" I asked the cop. He nodded.

"Dear Dev," I read, *"In case you were wondering, it was I who called the cops as I exited through the rear door. I knew what you were planning to do to me. By the time you get this I will be far away along with Rajan, but surely you know him well."* I shot a glance at the counter and, sure enough, Rajan was nowhere to be seen. *"He exchanged the bags. What you have in your hands is trash, just like my miserable life with you. Rajan fell in love with me and promised to help*

me escape. I hope you rot in jail. Life's like that. Love, Tara."

I crumpled the note and threw it away as the cop brought out a pair of handcuffs.

***

Tara sat in the waiting area at the airport, her shoulders slumped. A gentle voice announced the final call for the flight to Kathmandu. She sighed. It looked like Rajan would not turn up. The bastard's phone was switched off and she didn't know where he lived, or even his last name for that matter. She had only a few thousands with her. Just enough, perhaps, to go back to her hometown.

***

"Tickets please," called the TTE. "Please keep your ID ready."

He handed over his ticket and passport.

"Passport, huh? Don't get many of those, Mr... Rajan." The TTE flipped through his chart, found the name and ticked it off. "So, where are you off to?"

"Mangalore, and then I have a flight for Dubai."

"Well then, have a safe trip," said the TTE handing back the documents.

Raj sat back in his seat. Fortunately, the compartment was empty except for an old man nodding off in the opposite seat, a magazine open on his lap.

Raj hefted the maroon bag onto the seat beside him. It was time to count the eggs. Fifty lakhs were sufficient to start a new luxurious life. He opened the zipper and drew out a wad. His eyes grew wide. *Scrap paper! That Sai was a devil.* Raj looked around desperately. He was doomed.

The old man jerked awake looking bemused, then started reading his magazine.

'Life's like that,' read the caption on the cover.

You can sign up for my mailing list for exclusive content and new releases at www.kumarlauthor.com.

Dear Reader,

If you enjoyed this book, please take a few moments to leave a review on Amazon, Goodreads or your favourite site.

Thank you!

www.ingramcontent.com/pod-product-compliance
Lightning Source LLC
LaVergne TN
LVHW091609170726
843492LV00007B/2307

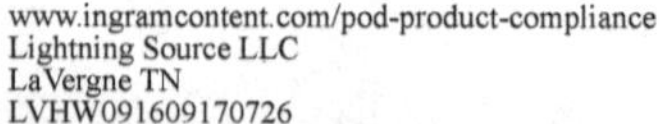